Dear Parent:
Your child's love of reading starts here!

Every child learns to read in a different way and at his or her own speed. Some go back and forth between reading levels and read favorite books again and again. Others read through each level in order. You can help your young reader improve and become more confident by encouraging his or her own interests and abilities. From books your child reads with you to the first books he or she reads alone, there are I Can Read Books for every stage of reading:

SHARED READING
Basic language, word repetition, and whimsical illustrations, ideal for sharing with your emergent reader

BEGINNING READING
Short sentences, familiar words, and simple concepts for children eager to read on their own

READING WITH HELP
Engaging stories, longer sentences, and language play for developing readers

READING ALONE
Complex plots, challenging vocabulary, and high-interest topics for the independent reader

I Can Read Books have introduced children to the joy of reading since 1957. Featuring award-winning authors and illustrators and a fabulous cast of beloved characters, I Can Read Books set the standard for beginning readers.

A lifetime of discovery begins with the magical words **"I Can Read!"**

Visit www.icanread.com for information
on enriching your child's reading experience.

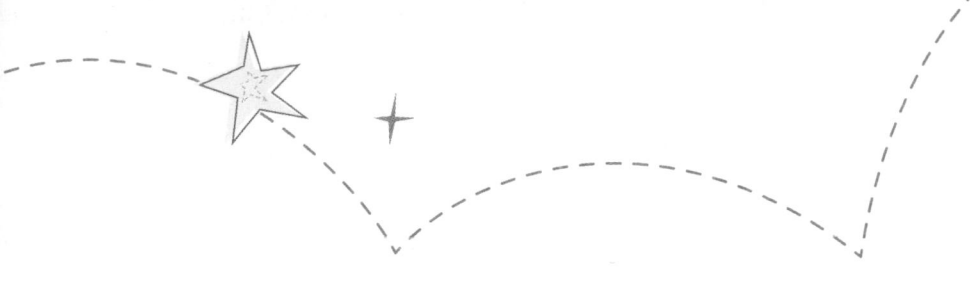

I Can Read® and I Can Read Book® are trademarks of HarperCollins Publishers.

My Little Pony: Pony Life: Royal Bake-Off

HASBRO and its logo, MY LITTLE PONY and all related characters are trademarks of Hasbro and are used with permission. © 2021 Hasbro.
All Rights Reserved. Printed in the United States of America.

Library of Congress Control Number: 2020946926
ISBN 978-0-06-303742-7

Book design by Elaine Lopez-Levine

22 23 24 25 LSCC 10 9 8 7 6 5 4 3 2 ❖ First Edition

I Can Read!

BEGINNING 1 READING

Royal Bake-Off

Based on the episode
"Princess Probz" written by Katie Chilson

HARPER
An Imprint of HarperCollinsPublishers

Pinkie Pie is making
a new dessert.
"It's an ice cream sundae!"
Pinkie Pie says.

Pinkie Pie is trying out

for a baking show.

"Baking show?"

Rainbow Dash asks.

"It's a competition!"

explains Pinkie Pie.

"And Princess Celestia
is the judge!" she adds.

But Pinkie Pie is a messy baker.
"She needs a clean workspace,"
Twilight Sparkle says.

Pinkie Pie is glad she
has Twilight Sparkle.
"I definitely need practice,"
Pinkie Pie laughs.

"To the kitchen!"

Pinkie Pie says.

In the kitchen, she mixes

a new dessert.

Pinkie Pie's friends huddle up.

"We have to help her,"

Twilight Sparkle says.

Twilight Sparkle looks at Pinkie Pie.

"Please tell me you have a plan,"
Twilight Sparkle says.

Pinkie Pie smiles.

"Step one: have fun!

That's the only step.

It's a one-step plan."

So Pinkie Pie's friends
come up with a new plan!

"Work carefully,"
Twilight Sparkle says.

"Be flashy.

Look the part.

And stay clean!"

"Turn it inside out, upside down!"

adds Twilight Sparkle.

That gives Pinkie Pie an idea!

She wants to bake upside-down cakes.

While her friends clean,

Pinkie Pie bakes the cakes.

But she slips on the clean floor . . .

And the cake explodes!

"We're in a sticky situation,"
Rainbow Dash says.

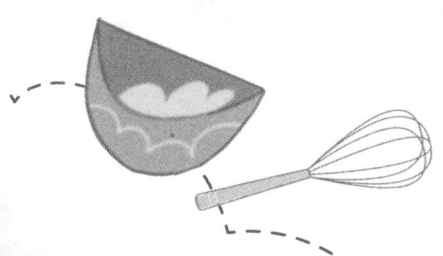

"Oh, no!" says Pinkie Pie.

"I wanted you to cheer me on."

But there's no time.

Pinkie Pie must go

to the competition alone.

"Pinkie Pie seems sad,"
Fluttershy says.
"This mess is my fault,"
Twilight Sparkle says.
"I just wanted to help."

"We have to make another
new plan," Applejack says.
"Let's eat!"

The baking competition begins!

"You have one chance,"

Princess Celestia tells Pinkie Pie.

"I'm baking upside-down cakes!"

Pinkie Pie says.

"I can do this."

Pinkie Pie is in her baking zone!
She tries to keep it clean,
and be flashy, and look the part,
but she can't help being herself.

She rushes around the kitchen, making a mess, but having fun. Soon, she presents her cake!

Just then, Pinkie Pie's friends burst in.

Princess Celestia takes a bite.

"This is the best cake!"

Princess Celestia tells Pinkie Pie.

"You must be on the show."

Pinkie Pie is surprised.

She thought it was a disaster.

"Your baking is top-notch,"

Princess Celestia says.

"But it's you who takes the cake."

Everyone cheers!

29

Pinkie Pie's friends apologize.

"I'm so sorry," Twilight Sparkle says.

"I tried to make you do it like me.

But it was perfectly you all along."

"I know you were trying to help.
But I can't help being me!
And I like it that way!"
Pinkie Pie says.